Five Bedtime Stories for Young Readers

By S. Brent Farley

Illustrated by Kiara Cryder

Story Titles

1. The Biggest Surprise Party of All

2. The Baby Bear and the Bumblebee

3. The Bamboozil

4. Thing-A-Ma-Jig

5. The Snowflake That Didn't Want to Melt

Published by S. Brent Farley in the United States of America.

Year Published: 2020

With Love,
S. Brent Farley

ISBN: 978-1-7348633-0-7 (Soft Cover Edition)

https://TopThoughts.shop

Five Bedtime Stories For Young Readers

This collection of original stories is dedicated to my seventeen grandchildren who as youngsters ignited my story-telling passion!

I would like to acknowledge my friend and mentor Taun Willis, an accomplished novelist who helped me launch my publication adventure!

Kiara Cryder enhanced the story with her clever and charming illustrations: thanks, Kiara for bringing the magic to life!

I also thank my first daughter Charlene Williams for her untiring help and encouragement in placing the illustrations and editing the stories!

For over fifty years my dear wife Janene has been a constant supporter and encourager for my enthusiastic endeavors in life: I thank her for her love and uplifting support!

The Biggest Surprise Party of All

Grandpa Anderson's birthday was coming, and Grandma wanted to surprise him with a birthday party. She had invited their children and grandchildren to come to the house at noon tomorrow. She would send Grandpa on an errand in the morning. When he came back for lunch, they would be ready for him. She had everything well planned.

Saturday morning arrived. Grandma wished him a "happy birthday!" At 10:00 in the morning she asked him to drive out to the country and bring their son Will and his family back for a birthday lunch. Grandpa happily got in the station wagon and started the engine. As he backed out of the driveway, he called to Grandma, "I'll be back at noon!"

At 10:15 five of the grandchildren arrived. They were going to help get ready for the party. Some were given the assignment to decorate the family room. Balloons had to be inflated, crepe paper strung here and there, and a "HAPPY BIRTHDAY" sign made.

Everyone had an assignment except Billy. He was the oldest of the grandchildren. Billy was a teenager and had his driver's license. "What can I do, Grandma?" asked Billy. He had in a set of earphones and was listening to his favorite music. (He usually had it turned up a bit too loud, so he didn't always hear what others were saying). Grandma smiled as she motioned for him to remove his earphones. "I've made a list of things you can do to help. All the people whose names I've written are waiting for their assignments this morning. I told them I'd have you drive by and tell them what they can do." She read down the list:

1. Grandpa wants his favorite pants for his birthday. They'll be ready now at the cleaners. Have your Uncle Charlie pick them up.
2. I'm going to give away a coat. Might as well take it on your way and drop it off at the used clothing store.
3. Send your cousin Johnny over to sweep the sand which is on the porch. That's where we'll have the birthday lunch.
4. Last week, Grandpa sat on his hat and smashed it. I've got a new one on hold. Ask your Uncle John to go to the store and pick up the new hat.
5. Tell your cousin Kevin to come over and string some wire across the front of the house. We'll hang Grandpa's birthday sign on it.

"You'd better hurry up. There isn't much time" Grandma said as Billy grabbed the list and ran out to the car. "Now don't you speed," Grandma called out as he started his engine. They could hear the car radio as he drove down the street. "That boy will be hard of hearing long before he reaches Grandpa's age," she declared.

Billy looked at the first item on the list and drove over to Uncle Charlie's place. As he pulled up, Uncle Charlie was just finishing mowing the lawn. "I'm in luck" thought Billy as he pulled over in front of the house. "This will save me some time. I won't even have to turn the engine off. I'll just yell from the car."

Uncle Charlie waved as he put the lawnmower on idle and turned down the power. "Hi Uncle Charlie. Grandma says you're waiting for an assignment for Grandpa's birthday party." Uncle Charlie nodded his head "yes" as the lawnmower idled. Billy called out, "Grandpa wants his favorite pants for his birthday. They're at the cleaners."

With the radio playing in the car and the lawnmower idling, Uncle Charlie didn't hear all that had been said. He called back to Billy, "Grandpa wants what?" "His **pants**," Billy yelled as he pulled out for the next errand on the list.

Uncle Charlie turned off the lawnmower. "That's very interesting. Grandpa wants to **dance** on his birthday. Well, if it's a dance he wants, it's a dance he'll get. I'll bet Grandma thought I'd bring over my favorite music collection to play. Well, I'll give them both a surprise. My friend Denny has a dance band. I'll bet I can hire them if it's not too late." So, Uncle Charlie called the leader of the band, and sure enough, the band was available. "Great," said Uncle Charlie. "Have them there about noon. It's sure to surprise them all."

As Billy was driving toward his cousin's house, he saw his friend Ed working in the front yard. Billy wanted Ed to see him driving, so he slowed down and honked the horn. Ed looked up and waved. "Where are you going?" called Ed. Billy put the brakes on and pulled over. "I'm helping Grandma get ready for Grandpa's birthday party. I have a list of things to do. Right now, I'm going to the store. Grandma's giving away a **coat**. Can't stop to talk. Lots of excitement this morning. I've got to hurry off; the party starts at noon."

Now Ed had his boom box turned up while he was working in the yard. And, Billy had the car radio on when he told Ed what he was doing. So, Ed didn't hear all that was said. "Well I'll be," he thought. "Billy's Grandpa is having a party at noon and his Grandma is giving away a **boat**. Wow. That is exciting! I'm going to call all of my friends. I'll bet they'd like a chance at winning a boat." With that, he turned off the boom box and hurried in the house to the phone.

When Billy got to his cousin Johnny's house, Johnny was playing with the dog. He would throw a frisbee and the dog would chase it. Sometimes he would catch it in the air. He was trained to bring the frisbee back and then sit until the frisbee was thrown again. While they were playing, the neighbor's dog was barking loudly because he wanted to play too. But he couldn't get out of the front yard.

Johnny called out to Billy, "Hey Billy - it's about time! What does Grandma want me to do?"

The neighbor's dog was barking more excitedly now. "She said she wants you to sweep the **sand which is** on the porch."

"Got it," yelled Johnny over the noise of the neighbor's dog. He waved as his cousin Billy drove away.

Johnny went into the house where his mother was reading. "Hey Mom. Billy just came by and said Grandma wants **sandwiches** on the porch."

"Well," his mother replied, "she doesn't give much notice, does she? I guess I'll have to order out. I hope they can make five dozen sandwiches in the next hour." She called the closest sandwich shop, and they said that for a surprise birthday for a grandpa, they would do it.

The next stop was at Uncle John's. Uncle John was a bit hard of hearing, but he wouldn't admit it. He would hear most of what was being said and then take a guess at the rest. Usually he did pretty good, but once in a while he guessed wrong. That's what happened this time. When Billy said, "Grandpa sat on his **hat** and smashed it," Uncle John thought to himself, "I didn't know Grandpa even owned a **cat**. It must have made him feel terrible to sit on his cat. I'll bet the little feller let out a screech before he died." When he tuned in again to what Billy was telling him, Billy said, "Grandma wants you to go to the store and pick up the new one." Uncle John thought he said, "Grandma wants you to go to the store and pick out a new one."

"Okay," answered Uncle John. As Billy drove away, Uncle John said to himself, "Grandma could have given me a little more time to make the choice." He drove over to the pet store and picked out a cute little yellow and black kitten. "Please deliver this about noon," he said as he gave them the address.

Billy thought to himself, "I'm making good time! I'll get everything taken care of just like Grandma asked me to do." After giving Grandma's old coat to the used clothing store, he started toward his cousin Kevin's home. Kevin lived about two miles away from Grandma and Grandpa's house. When he drove up, Kevin was putting air in the back tire of his bike. "Hi Billy," called out Kevin. "Hi Kevin," replied Billy. "Are you ready to help Grandma get ready for the surprise birthday party today at noon?"

"You bet I am. What does she want me to do?"

Looking at the last note on the list Grandma had given him, Billy answered, "She wants you to string some wire across the front of the house so that they can hang the birthday sign on it."

"She wants me to string wire across the front of the house?" Kevin asked to make sure he understood. "That's right," replied Billy.

"Well, I think I'll ride my bike over right now and get started. See you there." With that, Kevin hopped on his bike and began to pedal toward Grandma's house.

Billy had gotten the things on the list done early, so he decided to drive back home and take a shower. Then he would go over to Grandma's house for the excitement.

As Kevin was pedaling his bicycle, he passed a little neighbor boy who hollered out, "Hey Kevin, where ya goin'?"

"Kevin yelled back over his shoulder: I'm going to string some **wire** across the front of Grandma's house." Then he sped on. "Wow," said the little neighbor boy. He ran inside the house and yelled to his mother, "Kevin just went by on his bicycle and yelled that the front of his Grandma's house is on **fire**!"

"Are you sure?" asked his mother.

"That's what he yelled to me as he rode by" the boy answered.

"I wonder if anyone has called the fire department? Just to be safe, I'll make the call." With that his mother picked up the phone and dialed the emergency number. "Has anyone reported a fire at the Johnson's house?" she asked.

"No. We haven't received any calls about a fire today. What's the address?" The mother gave the address.

At the fire station, the alarm bell went off and the firemen put on their coats and ran to the fire engine. The fire station door opened and out rolled the fire engine with lights flashing and the siren wailing. It was followed by an ambulance with two paramedics.

At the police station, an officer jumped in his car and sped off to meet the fire engine at the house.

About this time the sandwich delivery car was pulling away from the shop with five dozen sandwiches for Grandma's front porch. As the driver turned left at the first intersection, he heard the loud horn of a fire truck along with the siren. He looked in his rear-view mirror and saw the flashing lights of the fire engine. He pulled over to the side and watched the fire truck speed by, followed by an ambulance. "Wow, I wonder what's going on?" the delivery boy said out loud. "It looks like they're going the same way I am," and he pulled out following at a safe distance.

Grandma was just taking a turkey out of the oven. She had prepared lots of food, lots of punch, and a big birthday cake for Grandpa. She was a very good cook and very well organized.

The grandchildren had decorated the living room and the porch. "I wonder where Johnny is," she said out loud to no one in particular. I'd like the sand swept off of the porch before I set the food out." Kevin was just climbing a ladder and putting a nail in the wood at the top of the porch so he could string a wire for the birthday sign.

At that point a van pulled up and some musicians began to get out. They carried their instruments as they walked up the sidewalk. "This looks like the place alright," the band leader said. "Let's set up over there."

While all of this was going on, Grandma was taking pies out of the oven and couldn't see what was going on out front. The grandchildren in the front yard were wide-eyed as they watched what was happening. "Grandma really planned a big party," one of them said. A group of teenagers had gathered on the front lawn in hopes of a chance at winning a new boat.

As Grandma was setting the last pie on the table, she heard the siren of a fire engine. "I wonder who's got a fire?" she said. "I hope it isn't anyone close by." The sound of the siren grew louder, and a horn blared loudly. "Oh dear," Grandma declared. "It sounds like it's coming to our street. I wonder if the neighbor's house is on fire?" With that she went out the back door to check the neighbors' homes on either side.

As the emergency vehicles turned onto Grandma's street, they saw the crowd gathered in front of the house. "There it is," a fireman called out. "I don't see any smoke. Maybe we're in time."

A police car sped in from the other direction and screeched to a halt across from the house. The officer jumped out of the car and began giving directions to the crowd that had gathered. "Stand back! Clear the way so the firemen can get through," he shouted. The grandchildren's eyes were as big as saucers.

The sandwich delivery car arrived and parked down the street. "Wow," said the driver. "This is the house where I'm supposed to deliver the sandwiches."

By this time the firemen had entered the front door and almost scared Grandma out of her wits. "Where's the fire?" the fire chief yelled.

"What fire?" Grandma answered with surprise.

"Someone called in and said your house was on fire."

"Lands sake, I hope not! I've been cooking all morning, but nothing's been burned. Whoever would have reported a fire at my house?"

"If it's alright, we'll just look around and make sure everything's okay" said the fireman. "It sounds like a false alarm." They began looking around the house as Grandma went to the front door. When she saw the crowd outside, she nearly fainted. "Who are all these people?"

"I don't know," replied one of the grandchildren. "But everyone's excited! Is this all part of Grandpa's surprise party?"

By this time all the children and grandchildren had arrived and had to park down the street because of the crowd. As they ran to the house and saw the fire engine and the ambulance and the police car, they thought something was wrong with Grandma or Grandpa. "Oh dear," they said. "Who's going to the hospital?"

Well, when everything was sorted out, things calmed down a bit. The emergency people were invited to have some food before they returned to work. After all, with Grandma's cooking and five dozen sandwiches, there was plenty for all - including the teenagers who had gathered around for the giveaway of a new boat. In fact, the firemen were nice enough to give a tour of the fire engine and allowed the cousins to take photos holding the fire hose and wearing the fire helmets!

Billy arrived about the same time as Grandpa returned with Will's family from the country. The firemen had decided to leave their lights flashing until Grandpa arrived. They thought it would add to the party atmosphere. When Grandpa pulled in the driveway and got out of his car, the band started up and **everyone yelled**...

Surprise!

Then they sang "Happy Birthday"

Grandpa went to Grandma and gave her a hug. "I don't know how you pulled this off, but it's the biggest surprise I've ever had." "Me too," Grandma replied quietly. Billy simply said: "Wow, this is really great!"

It turned out to be the best party Grandpa ever had, and the most talked about in the family for years to come. No one was disappointed, except for the group of teenagers who didn't get a chance at winning a new boat. But they stayed and enjoyed the food. They even danced for a while.

That left just one thing: the delivery of the little kitten. It arrived late, toward the end of the party. Grandpa had never had a kitten of his own. When he took it in his hands, it began to purr, and Grandpa broke out with a big smile. He winked at Grandma and wondered again how she could have planned such a big surprise birthday party. Nobody ever figured it out - including Grandma and Billy.

The End

The Baby Bear and the Bumblebee

Once upon a time in a beautiful forest far away, there lived a baby bear. Her name was "Cinnamon." She was furry and cuddly and very cute.She was born in a cave and stayed close to her mother. As she began to grow, she began to play baby bear games inside the cave. One summer day she asked her mother if she could explore outside the cave and her mother said "yes, but don't wander too far away. I want you to be safe." Cinnamon stepped outside into the bright sunshine and began to explore a beautiful world. It was fun to be outside. Every day from then on, she spent more and more time outdoors. She felt very safe.

One day on a warm, sunny afternoon Cinnamon was sitting outside while her mother took a nap in the cave. It was very quiet. She was looking at a pine tree when she heard a buzzing sound behind her. She turned her head just in time to spot a yellow bumblebee. It was the first time she had ever seen a bee. It flew lazily in the air as if it had nowhere to go. Curious, Cinnamon stood up and moved toward the bumblebee. As soon as she did, it flew a little farther away. Cinnamon followed, and together they moved down the mountainside, as if playing "hide and seek."

Cinnamon didn't see the mountain lion, but the mountain lion heard Cinnamon playing on the forest floor. On this particular day, Cinnamon had wandered farther away from the cave than she had ever been before. The sneaky mountain lion crouched down and moved slowly toward the sounds Cinnamon was making. It was almost impossible for Cinnamon to see her as the lion crept closer and closer.

Back in the cave, the mother bear awakened and looked around for her baby. When she couldn't find her, she stood up and slowly walked outside. As her eyes got used to the sunlight, she saw movement off in the distance in the forest ferns under a big pine tree. It was her baby playing. Then she spotted the mountain lion crouched at the side of a rock near the tree. It was getting ready to leap out at her baby bear.

Cinnamon was so busy playing make-believe games that she was not aware of the danger close by. She was having fun, grunting baby bear grunts as she ran back and forth among the ferns. Suddenly she heard a great roar from the cave. She froze in her tracks, for she knew that something was very wrong. She had never heard her mother roar like that. There really was danger, and Cinnamon was frightened.

The mother bear began to run toward the ferns, and she roared again. Cinnamon quickly looked around. It was then that she saw the eyes of the mountain lion staring straight at her. What should she do? She couldn't run up the tree because the lion was too close to it. Should she run toward her mother, or hold very still right where she was? She quickly decided to turn and run.

The mountain lion knew she could easily catch the baby bear. But the crashing noise of the huge mother running toward them made her very nervous. The roars from the mother bear told the mountain lion that she had better get out of there fast. She quickly decided not to stay. No dinner was worth this. As she turned to run, she slipped on a loose rock. By now the mother bear was so close that she swung her mighty paw at the lion. The lion felt the wind of the paw as it barely missed her. She leaped and ran for her life. She ran and ran and never stopped running until she was out of the valley and very far away.

Cinnamon now knew why her mother had told her not to get too far away from home. Home was a safe place. She was glad to be at the side of her mother again. From then on, Cinnamon always asked her mother if she could play, and she always stayed close enough to the cave so that her mother could protect her. She would wait until she was more grown up before she wandered away again.

The rest of the summer was a happy adventure. Cinnamon learned about the whole valley as she explored with her mother. She learned how to look for food. They would eat berries and dig roots from plants. One time Cinnamon even watched her mother catch a fish from the beautiful stream that ran through their valley. It provided a tasty meal.

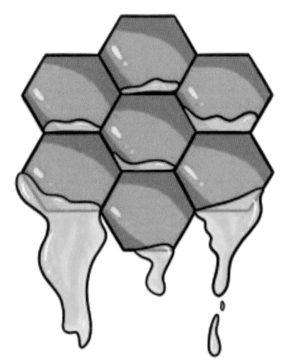

The best treat of all, however, was the first time Cinnamon tasted honey. It came from a honeycomb in the hollow of an old tree trunk. As they ate, the bees were buzzing loudly. They darted all around the two bears. But the thick fur of the bears protected them from the bees. The honeybees reminded Cinnamon of the larger bee she had been following on the day the mountain lion had sneaked up on her.

By the end of the summer, Cinnamon had grown quite a bit. She was happy in their little valley. But one evening, everything suddenly changed. She and her mother were sound asleep in their cave. Late in the night, the sky suddenly lit up brighter than day as a flash of lightning struck the huge, old pine tree just down from their cave. A crash of thunder followed that shook the air. The tree caught on fire and the flames leaped up the branches.

The wind was blowing and soon the fire had spread until the dry valley was ablaze. The flames grew and raced up the mountain toward their cave.

Mother told Cinnamon to run as fast as she could away from the fire. Cinnamon tried to run with her mother, but the wind changed direction and blew thick smoke all around them. She got lost, and her eyes burned from the smoke. She ran wildly trying to get away from the heat and the smoke.

Suddenly she fell down a bank and landed in cold water. She knew it was the stream where her mother had caught fish for dinner. It felt so good to be protected from the heat that she huddled under the bank of the stream while the fire raged all around. That's what saved her life.

When morning came, the fire had burned over the entire valley. It was black and smoky all around, but Cinnamon was alive. She walked carefully down the edge of the stream, for it was too hot to walk through the forest. She traveled for a long time until she was in a new valley that had not been in the path of the fire. She left the water and walked again on the forest floor. She was so tired that she laid down under the branches of a large bush and fell fast asleep.

It was noon when Cinnamon awoke. She looked around for her mother, hoping the fire in the night had only been a bad dream. But it wasn't a dream. She began to cry softly as she realized that the fire had really happened. What would she do now? What could she do? At this very moment, she thought she heard her named hummed softly: "Cinn-a-monnnnnnnnnn." She looked around and saw no one. She must be imagining things. Then she heard it again. She was not imaging anything! She looked toward the sound and saw a bumblebee buzzing above her head.

"Did you call my name," asked the little bear?

"That I did," replied the bumblebee.

"How did you know my name?" she asked.

"I learned it when you were born," replied the bumblebee. "I was there."

"Do you have a name?"

"Yes, I do. My name is `Bumble.' I've had my eye on you for a long time."

Cinnamon remembered the time she had followed a bumble bee and had wandered away from the cave. She asked, "Were you the one I followed that day when the mountain lion wandered into our valley?

"Yes," Bumble replied.

"Then it was your fault I nearly became the lion's dinner!"

"No, it wasn't. I was the one who saved you! When I saw the mountain lion sneaking up, I flew quickly back to the cave and awakened your mother. It was I who showed her the danger you were in. She thanked me later for stinging her on the ear to wake her up."

"My mother is gone now," said Cinnamon sadly. "We had a terrible fire last night and I got lost trying to escape with her. Our valley is ruined and I'm all alone. I don't know what to do."

"That's why I'm here," answered Bumble. "I can help you."

"But you're so little! What can you do to help?"

"Just follow me and see," said Bumble. With that, the bumblebee started to fly off through the forest. Cinnamon nearly had to run to keep up. She didn't know where they were going, but Bumble was the only friend she had right now.

They came to a patch of fresh berries. She realized how hungry she was and looked around for Bumble. "Where are you, Bumble?" she called.

"Right here," answered Bumble as he sat on a huge, ripe berry close by. "It's time for lunch. Eat until you're full, and then we'll continue." While she ate, Bumble flew among the nearby flowers gathering food for himself. Cinnamon filled her tummy completely!

She was beginning to feel good again. Bumble landed on her nose and said gently, "It's time to move on." "Where are you leading me?" she asked. Bumble didn't reply, but just flew on ahead. They traveled together the rest of the afternoon, a baby bear and a bumblebee. Whoever would have imagined such a pair?

At the end of the new valley they stopped to drink from a pond.

After a rest, they started up a trail toward a mountain pass. When they were near to the pass, Bumble stopped. "If you go through that pass, you'll know what to do," he said to Cinnamon.

"Are you leaving me?" Cinnamon asked with alarm.

"No. I'm not leaving you. I'm leading you, but now I want you to go first. I'll follow close behind."

"Alright," said Cinnamon, "but how will I know you're following?"

"Just listen carefully as you go, and you'll be able to hear me humming close by. Now hurry along."

Cinnamon hurried up the trail that led to the pass. Occasionally, she would stop and listen for Bumble's hum. When she heard him, she would move ahead. When she reached the top of the pass, she could hardly believe what she was seeing. Sitting beneath a large pine tree just a little way in front of her was her mother. Cinnamon called out, and the two bears ran to each other. What a happy moment it was when they were reunited! "Oh mother," Cinnamon cried, "I thought I had lost you. I was so afraid."

"And I was worried about you," replied her mother. "But Bumble told me he would look for you and if he found you, he would lead you back to me. Bumble can fly, and he can look down from high up in the air. I'm so glad he found you." At that very moment, Bumble landed on a flower next to Cinnamon. He buzzed a happy buzz, then off he flew.

"Where is Bumble going now?" Cinnamon asked.

"Oh, he has a home of his own with other bumblebees," replied the mother bear. "But he'll be back from time to time. Somehow he always knows when to show up."

The fall was a wonderful season for Bumble and her mother. As the leaves changed colors, they found a new home.

Many forest animals and birds made friends with them as they prepared for the coming winter. When it was time to hibernate, Bumble settled down in a soft bed of pine boughs and leaves in a brand-new cave. As she was getting sleepy, she heard a familiar hum. She smiled as Bumble landed on her nose. "Oh, that tickles," she said. "Have you come to say goodnight before I go to sleep for the winter?"

"Yes, I have," said Bumble. "Would you like to visit for a while before you go to sleep?"

"I would like that," replied Cinnamon with a yawn. "I want to thank you for helping me. It was very kind of you." She paused a few moments, and then continued. "You know, I've been wondering about something. The lion and the forest fire sometimes come back in my mind and I'm afraid to go to sleep. Why did they have to happen?"

"I don't know the answer to that," replied Bumble. "But I do know a secret that can help you get to sleep. Did you learn anything good from those experiences?"

"Oh yes," replied Bumble. "I learned many good things. I learned how important it is to obey good rules. I learned how much I enjoy being alive, and how I love my mother. And, I learned how much help a good friend like you can give."

"And how do you feel when you think about the good things?"

"I feel happy inside."

"And that's the secret," replied Bumble. Don't think about the bad things that have happened. Think about the good things you learned, and let the happy thoughts crowd out the bad ones. Then you'll be able to go to sleep. That's what I learned a long time ago. Let the happy thoughts run through your mind . . .."

But Cinnamon was already asleep with a pleasant look on her face.

THE END

THE BAMBOOZIL

Note: (A "Whoozil" is a friendly imaginary creature that looks just like you want it to look. A "Bamboozil" is . . . well, that's what this poem is about.)

There once was a Whoozil
Who found a "Bamboozil"
And didn't know quite what it was;
So, he took it back home
And sat down alone
To figure out just what it does.

He found you could roll it,
Push it or pull it,
Or twirl it around overhead;
You could bounce it or bump it
Or slide it and jump it,
Or sleep on it just like a bed.

You could bend it and shape it,
Float it or sail it,
Or fly it by adding some wings;
You could twist it and turn it,
Or study to learn it,
Then make lots of curious things.

"What a wonderful, wonderful toy I have found!
It works in the water, the air, or on ground!
There's nothing to think of that it doesn't do;
From morning through nighttime, the fun's nev-
er through.
I like it so much that I can't put it down -
Tomorrow I'll take it and show it in town."

Next day in the town
He showed it around
And the Whoozils all thought it was great!
A circus was formed
And the Whoozil performed
Every act the "Bamboozil" could make.

It would swing, it would fly,
It would spin low and high,
It would form into dozens of shapes:
Like lions and bees,
Alligators and fleas,
And even gorillas and apes.

It could flash like a fire
And dance on a wire
Like lazars afloat on a breeze;
It could roar with a sound
That would shake the whole ground,
Or sniffle and sound like a sneeze.

The Whoozil was proud
That they drew such a crowd,
They were headed for glory and fame -
'Til a little old man
Hobbled up to the stand
And said, "Bill Bamboozil's my name."

"You've done very fine
With something that's mine!
When I lost it, my life became dim.
But I've found it now,
And I think somehow
It will make me happy again."

With a wink of his eye
He said, "goodbye,"
And started to walk on his way.
The "Bamboozil" followed,
The Whoozil just swallowed,
Then called out, "What is it today?"

"It is what it was,
And it does what it does,
Quite often with exaggeration!
But you'll soon understand
That the reason it's grand
Is because it's *imagination*!

He watched them depart,
Then thought in his heart
"I'm not going to stay here alone;
I'll go home today
And start right away
To develop one of my own!"

THE END.

THING-A-MA-JIG

It was late in the afternoon when the delivery truck pulled up to the factory. The boxes were unloaded and taken to a little room with small windows around the top. A worker opened each box and laid the contents on a table. Then he left and closed the door behind him.

There were many noises that came from inside the factory. Bangs and rattles, and screeching metal sounds mixed in with the voices of the workers. At the end of the day, a long whistle blew three times, and all the sounds died out as the people left. It soon became very quiet in the factory.

When evening arrived, stars began winking their lights in the darkened sky. They were signaling for the moon to rise. It was a beautiful, full moon that came up from behind the mountain.

23

When its light shined through the small windows, that's when the magic began. It was a moment of magic that only happens once every twenty years. This was the night. In the next few minutes, things without life could suddenly speak and see and hear. They could talk to each other just like people. For a little while, they could actually think. But the people would never know.

On the table inside the little room, the items that had been delivered noticed that tools hung all around the walls. They had become part of a tool room, and they were there to replace some of the old, worn out tools. Suddenly, the magic began! "Hello everybody," a voice called out. "I think we should have some introductions from our new guests. You there, on the end. Please introduce yourself."

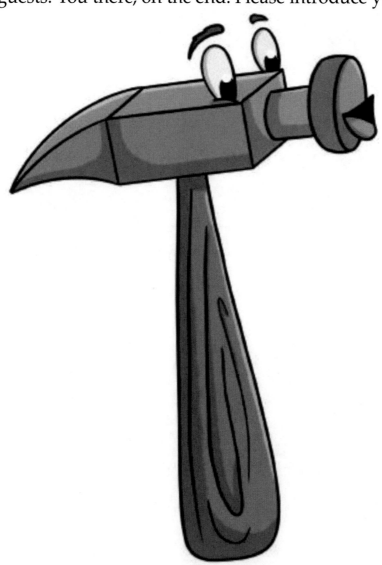

On the end of the table lay a shiny new hammer. It said, "Hello. I'm happy to be here. As you can see, I'm a hammer. My job is to pound on things. I can drive nails into wood, bend things, pound out dents...I'm a very useful tool and I'm anxious to begin work."

"That's wonderful," said the leader. He looked in another direction. "And how about you?"

"I'm a wrench. I turn things. I can loosen to help take things apart or tighten up to help put things together."

By now the new arrivals were anxious to talk and didn't need an invitation.

"I'm a screwdriver," explained the next item on the table. It had a clear, orange handle.

"I'm very useful also. I can turn screws that fasten things together, like cupboards and shelves."

"And I'm a saw. I'm used to cut things apart. Those things are then put together to build something nice for others!

The last item on the delivery table sat in a clear plastic box. It didn't speak up. Finally, the leader prompted, "And how about you? What do you do?"

The item bashfully replied, "I don't know. I'm not sure what I am or what I can do. I'm very sorry."

The leader of the tools replied, "Well, don't feel badly. I'm sure there's a use for you. Until you find out what you are and what you are good for, we'll just call you a `thing-a-ma-jig.' How's that for a name? `Thing-a-ma-jig.'" The other tools nodded their approval.

The leader continued, "On behalf of all the other tools in the factory, we'd like to welcome you to our group. You'll be replacing some of the older ones tomorrow.

I'd like you to know that this is quite a distinguished group. Some of these tools might even be considered heroes. I'd like to invite those who are retiring to tell their stories. You're first, Mr. Hammer."

The handle of the old hammer was scarred and cracked on one side, but the metal head was still strong and proud. It was obvious to the new tools on the table that Mr. Hammer had seen many years of hard work.

He replied: "I'm very glad to welcome the new tools and `thing-a-ma-jig.' I've helped to build wagons and fences, houses and barns, and a host of other things. I remember one time in my younger days when a new family needed help fast. A large tree had been blown over by the wind. As it fell, one of its limbs knocked a hole in the roof. A rainstorm was coming, and if the hole was not patched very quickly, the rainwater would come inside the home and damage the furnishings. I was hanging on a hook in the shed at the time.

The father came running in and grabbed me and a bunch of nails. He carried a ladder to the side of the house. With the wind still blowing, he carried a large piece of wood up the ladder and onto the roof. I was used to hammer the nails that fastened the wood over the hole. Shingles were hastily nailed over the plank. When we got back down the ladder, there was just enough time to get inside the house before the rain started to pour. It rained hard for hours, but the patch held and protected the inside of the home. A couple of days later, when things had dried out, we went back up and fixed the roof proper. I heard the father say, "if it hadn't been for my trusty hammer, we'd have been in real trouble."

Thing-a-ma-jig was very impressed. She thought to herself, "I wish I could do something important to help someone else. But I'm so small, and such a different shape than all the others. I just don't feel like I fit in. How can I be helpful to anyone for anything?"

The wrench was probably the oldest tool of the bunch. He still looked sturdy and strong, though he was a little rusty. Thing-a-ma-jig wondered what services he had performed for others over the years.

He began to speak. "I'm proud of the life I have enjoyed. I've seen many places and worked for many people. I've seen good times and bad times. Through it all, I've managed to do my jobs faithfully. I think the job I am most proud of was the time I helped an orphanage. It was many years ago. An old building was fixed up to house little children until they were adopted. Before it could be used, it needed heat. I helped build a boiler to circulate hot steam in order to keep the place warm. There were a lot of bolts and nuts that had to be in place. We did a right nice job. When the boiler was completed and started up, it circulated heat just fine. A lot of children enjoyed the warmth during the winter months while they waited to join families who wanted them. I think that's one of the things I feel best about in my life."

Thing-a-ma-jig felt a tear coming as she thought about the contribution the wrench had made. "Oh, I hope I can do something like that to help others. I wonder what I'll be and what I'll do."

The wrench continued: "Do you remember those times, Mr. Screwdriver?"

"Oh, indeed I do. Like you, I've been many places and done many things. Perhaps the biggest job I ever worked on was the construction of a large business building that towered over all the other buildings of the city. But the job I felt best about had to do with that orphanage. I was used to help put Christmas toys together. There were tricycles and bicycles, and a whole lot of games. There were rocking horses and little chairs. I'll never forget the look of happiness on the children's faces on Christmas morning. That made me feel good all over. It's a wonderful feeling to do work that makes others happy."

The leader noticed a look of sadness on Thing-a-ma-jig's face. "What's wrong, little Thing-a-ma-jig? You should be happy!"

"Oh, I am happy," replied Thing-a-ma-jig. "I'm happy for what the others have done. But what am I going to become? I'm so little. I don't know what I'm good for. Will I ever do something important? I'm afraid I'll never be as good as the rest of you."

The leader chuckled with understanding. "We know how you feel. We've all felt that way at one time or another. It's natural to wonder what you'll become." (The other tools nodded in agreement).

"Don't worry now. Just be your best and something good will come along. You'll see."

"Thing-a-ma-jig," said the leader with a kindly look, "I think you'd be interested in meeting an old friend of ours whom we respect very much. Look over in the corner of that cupboard over there."

Thing-a-ma-jig looked in the direction of the cupboard and saw a tired old pipe wrench. It had been lying there quietly the whole time. Everyone's attention focused on him. As he began to speak slowly about his "good old days," he brightened up , straightened up, and seemed to take on a younger appearance.

"I've done a lot of work in many places. I've helped make life good for a lot of people. One day a water pipe was leaking in a home. If it wasn't fixed, the basement would have been flooded. I was the one that tightened the connection and stopped the leak. You might say that I `saved the day.' But the strain of the final turn was so great that I broke. I've not felt very useful since then, but my friends have treated me with respect. They let me stay here where I can enjoy their company. That makes me feel important, even though I can't keep doing the things I used to do. At least I can still associate with my friends and feel their respect."

Thing-a-ma-jig began to smile as a new tear formed. She was learning a good lesson. She watched as the wrench slowly settled back into his comfortable position.

She listened as the next tool, a hack saw, began to speak.

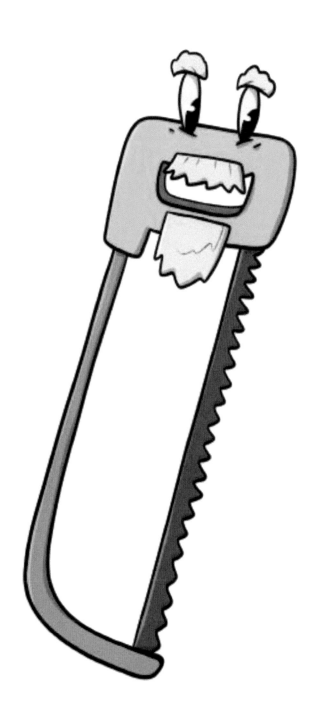

"I've been used to help build many homes. I cut through metal to make it the right size, like the pipes that make it possible for homes to have running water. Of course, without the other tools, the houses couldn't have been built. It's a team effort. That's what I've done all my life. The last project I helped with was the construction of a fire station. I can look back on a good life."

The next morning when the factory opened, it became noisy again from the workers returning. The door to the tool room swung wide as two men walked into the room. They were talking as they entered.

"Well, the project is ready. They've completed the remodel on the fire station and they're ready for the new ambulance to be delivered. The opening ceremonies are this morning. They would like it to arrive at 10:00 a.m. with the siren going.

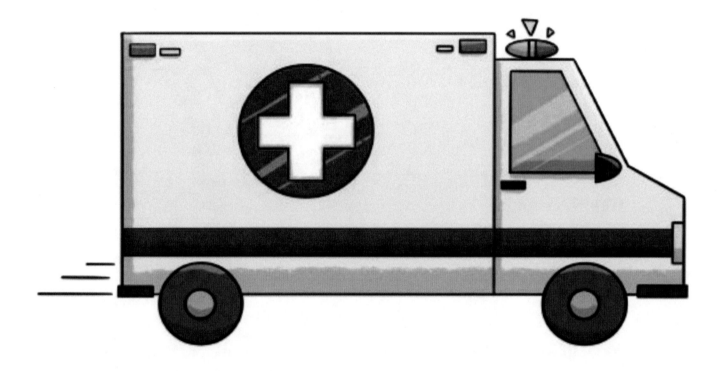

As you know, the only problem was that the keys were lost. A new set was ordered two days ago. Bob, will you drive it over?"

"Yes, I will be happy to," replied Bob. "That will be exciting! All I need is that valuable set of keys. Can't run an emergency vehicle without the keys!"

The factory foreman said, "They're right over there with the new tools that were delivered yesterday." He walked right up to Thing-a-ma-jig and picked her up. "Here's your ticket to a lot of valuable service for a lot of valuable and needy folks ahead!"

Thing-a-ma-jig now knew what she was! She was the key to a new ambulance! And, she had a twin sister that she hadn't noticed in the paper underneath her in the same box she had arrived in. They would work together to help others for the rest of their lives. It would be in a different way than the other tools, but she now knew that she was an important part of a team!

As Bob left the tool room with the new set of keys in his hand, a moment of magic returned as all of the tools smiled one last time and winked at Thing-a-ma-jig.

THE SNOWFLAKE THAT DIDN'T WANT TO MELT

Have you ever seen a mountain all covered with snow? Or a snow-capped peak, with just the top showing white? Have you ever thrown a snowball, or made a snowman by packing snow and rolling it through more snow until it grows bigger and bigger? Or ridden a sled down a trail packed with cold, slick snow?

Do you know that without little snowflakes, none of this would be possible? No mountains covered with snow, no snowballs or snowmen - because these bigger things are made up by a whole bunch of little snowflakes joining together. It's kind of like how the world is made up by a whole bunch of people. Without the people, there wouldn't be any nations. Nations begin with little children who grow up to be adults.

It's the little things that make bigger things possible. This story is about the adventures of one little snowflake by the name of "Crystal."

Crystal was born at the North Pole. Her mother was a cloud. When the cloud got cold, the moisture it carried began to form into tiny ice crystals. (If you could see these ice crystals, they would be beautiful to look at. Some of them are shaped like shiny stars). It took one hundred crystals joining together to make this particular snowflake.

It was December when Crystal took her first ride on the wind. She dropped from the cloud and sailed with ease. She learned that she could float, or twirl, or spin around like a dancer in the sky. It was great fun to be alive. She wanted to go places and see different sights. She wanted to try doing different things to find out what she liked the best. She asked the wind upon which she rode how far it would take her.

"How far do you want to go?" replied the wind.

"I don't really know. The world is so big and I'm so little. How far can I go?"

"Well," said the wind, "first you have to learn about yourself. It will take a long time to before you know how much you can do and how far you can go. The first thing you must know is what you are. You're a snowflake. As long as you stay cold, you will remain a snowflake. If you ever warm up, you will melt and turn into water. I'd suggest you visit some cold places and see where snowflakes live. Would you like to take a trip?"

"Sure," said Crystal. "Will you watch out for me and help me get around?"
"That's a promise," said the wind. "Now hang on and I'll take you to the first stop." With that, the wind gave an extra puff and sent Crystal hurling through the sky with thousands of other snowflakes.

When she landed, she was on top of an iceberg. The wind settled to a breeze. "What are those creatures?" she asked?

"Those are penguins," whispered the wind. Crystal watched them marching around. They sort of waddled as they walked. They were black and white as if dressed in tuxedo suits. "Can I go down closer?"

"Sure," answered the wind as it gently carried her down to the ground. Just stay out of the way as they walk. When she lit, a penguin was passing by. She had to look up from the ground. It looked much larger now. "Wow," said Crystal. "I didn't know until now how big penguins are."

"Well, if you like it here, you can stay. Just freeze and become a part of an iceberg. Then you can watch the penguins as they play. They might even use your iceberg as a slippery slide.

That would be fun. But, you don't have to decide that now."

"Are penguins the biggest things alive?"

"No, chuckled the wind. You want to see `big'? Just come with me."

With that, the wind picked her up and whisked her to the edge of an island. "Look over there in that valley."

Crystal saw her first polar bear. It was a magnificent creature with thick white fur. "Let's take a closer look," whispered the wind, and with that it carried Crystal to a mound of snow right next to the polar bear. Crystal could hardly believe her eyes. It was a beautiful animal. It was also very big! It walked slowly to a snowbank and then got down and rolled back and forth. Crystal almost laughed. It was fun watching this huge animal.

"Are there other kinds of animals," Chrystal asked?

"More than you can ever have time to learn about. The world is a very big place, and there are many animals in many places."

"Can I see them all?" asked Crystal.

"I'm afraid you can't. Remember, you are a snowflake and you live in a cold place. So, the only animals you can see are those that live in cold places. That's so you won't melt; that is, unless you want to."

Crystal interrupted, "I never want to melt. I want to stay like I am forever!"

"We'll see," replied the wind. "Now, as I was saying, you live in a cold place, so the animals you see will be different than the animals that live in hot places. Would you like to see more?"

"Oh yes; I'd like to see as much as I can. Just don't ever take me where I will melt."

The wind blew up a gust and Crystal began to flutter around. Then with a "Wheeee" she took off like she was riding on a roller coaster. She was whisked over ice bergs and across frozen water. She loved every minute of it. There were new places to see and new things to learn. She was happy to be in cold places. She felt soooo good.

As she sailed through the air, new sights came into view. The wind began to lower her toward another island with a beautiful, wintry forest. Then with a quick swoop, it tossed her high up in the air and then let her float downward. When she landed, she was on a pine tree right in the middle of a herd of reindeer. Some of them had horns on their heads.

She wiggled and fell to a lower branch so that she could see better.

"Oh, this is exciting" she thought to herself. "Maybe I'll stay here and become a part of this beautiful winter forest."

The sun was shining now, but the air was so cold that it kept her frozen. "I don't ever want to melt" she said again. "This is so much fun just being who I am."

Crystal spent the next few days just learning about the forest. She liked to learn about new things. Doing new things was very exciting. By now she had learned that she didn't need to ask for help every time she wanted to go somewhere. Whenever the wind started, she could turn a certain way and sail like a kite. She could go anywhere she wanted, anytime she wanted when the wind was blowing. But soon she was about to learn a different and very important lesson.

Crystal sailed to a new valley. There were animals there called "Caribou." They were big animals, and she wanted to see them up close. As she landed on their trail, a wolf howled in the distance. This scared the Caribou and they began to run down the trail. Crystal tried to get out of the way, but the wind wasn't blowing anymore. "Oh, I shouldn't have gotten so close," she thought as the animals thundered toward her. "I should have asked the wind if I would be safe. I should have let the wind set me down somewhere else." She tried one last time to get out of the way, but the wind wasn't there. Crystal felt the whole ground shake as the animals ran by. She knew that if she was stepped on, she would be crushed.

Suddenly a hoof struck a rock and sent it flying. Crystal hadn't known that she had landed on this very rock! She clung on with all of her might as it went spinning through the air, but she couldn't hold on for very long. Off she flew, twirling through the air. It was a gust of wind that caught her and carried her safely away.

"Whew! That was close," cried the snowflake. She was still shaking. "What happened?"

"You went somewhere you shouldn't have gone. You chose to get too close to something that was dangerous. You've learned to do many things on your own. You need to learn that there are some things you shouldn't do."

"I'll be more careful from now on. And thanks for showing up at the right time to save me."

"You're welcome," replied the wind. "You are worth it. Is there anything else I can do for you before I leave?"

"I think so." Crystal thought for a while. "Is there any other cold place you think I should visit? Is there something I haven't done or seen that would be good for me?"

"Perhaps there is. I think you are ready for a new experience. Hang on."

It was good to be riding again on the wind. Crystal had learned to trust it.

They sailed for a long time. Lights appeared below. The wind explained that they were flying over a town. In the town were people.

"Are people animals?" Crystal asked.

"No, people are different from animals. Just watch them and you'll learn something. Now let go and float to the ground with the other snowflakes. I'll be back soon to find out what you've learned."

Crystal let go and became a part of a gentle snowstorm. She landed at the side of a frozen pond. It was dark at the pond, but she could see the lights coming from around the town. She watched the lights and wondered what people were like. While she was thinking, the lights began to go off one by one. Soon she was asleep.

When morning came it was frosty and cold - just the way Crystal liked it. She still wondered what people would look like. As she was trying to imagine, she heard a sound she had never heard before. It was not a scary sound at all. It was a happy sound. It was the sound of children laughing. "This must be the people coming," she thought as she looked around excitedly. She was right. It was Saturday morning and the children were out of school. They were running and sliding in the snow. They made snowballs and snowmen. Some had sleds that they pulled up the hill. Then they would get on top of the sleds and slide back down the hill with squeals of delight. Others put on ice skates and slid across the frozen pond. Crystal watched with excitement as they played all day long.

When evening came, she heard another new sound. It was a group of people singing Christmas carols. There were little people and big people all mixed together. Their singing made her feel good inside. "I think I'm going to like people a lot," decided Crystal. "Perhaps I'll stay here forever."

She spent the entire winter at the edge of the town. She loved it when the children would come out to play. But deep inside she was beginning to feel like moving on.

One morning the wind dropped by for a visit. "Hi Crystal. How have you enjoyed your visit in the town?"

"I have enjoyed it very much. So far, it's the best place I've ever been. You know, I've been thinking about where I've been and what I've done." Then she paused thoughtfully.

"Go on, whispered the wind. I'm listening."

"Well," Crystal replied, "I liked it when I was born at the North Pole and first sailed in the wind. I thought I would be happy to stay right there. But if I had stayed there, I would never have seen the penguins or the polar bear. If I had become a part of the iceberg by the polar bear, I would not have seen the winter forest with its animals. And if I had stayed in the winter forest, I would never have seen the people. What if I had stopped learning about places and things and decided to stay in one spot. I could have missed out on so much."

The wind smiled and sighed. "You have learned a valuable lesson, Crystal. You have discovered that life is more than a place where you live. It is a wonderful journey with lots of places to go and lots of things to learn."

"Is there something else I can learn?" asked Crystal. "Have I seen everything I can see?"

"If you never want to melt, then you've seen all you can see, and you've learned all you can learn."

"Then I can't stay the way I am? Is that right?"

"I didn't say that. You can stay just the way you are. But it won't be as fun."

"I didn't think I would ever want to melt. But maybe I didn't understand. What will happen if I melt?"

The wind replied quietly: "then you will continue on your journey like millions of other snowflakes. There is always something to look forward to."

"Can I see other places that are not cold? I've tried to imagine what they are like. Will I still be me if I melt? Will I still be happy?"

"Yes," replied the wind. "You will still be you. And you will have new opportunities beyond your dreams. You will be happier than ever before. All of the things you have done so far are just the beginning."

"Are you sure?" Crystal asked.

"I'm very sure. I've watched it happen many, many times."

"Then I'll go," said Crystal. "How do I begin?"

"Do you remember the first time you rode on my back when you fell from the cloud?"

"I do," replied Crystal.

"When spring arrives and the sun begins to warm the earth, just look up and smile. You will find that you will like the warmth. Then hang on for another ride."

"Will I ever see you again?" asked Crystal.

"Absolutely," replied the wind. "I blow all over the earth. I guarantee that we'll be together again. See you around." With a little puff, the wind was gone. Crystal sighed. She was a little sad to be leaving, but very anxious to learn new things and see other places.

Spring came just like the wind had said. The snow all around her began to melt. It seemed like it was the normal thing to do. She looked up in the sky and saw the sun shining. For the first time she felt warm. She was surprised by how good it felt.

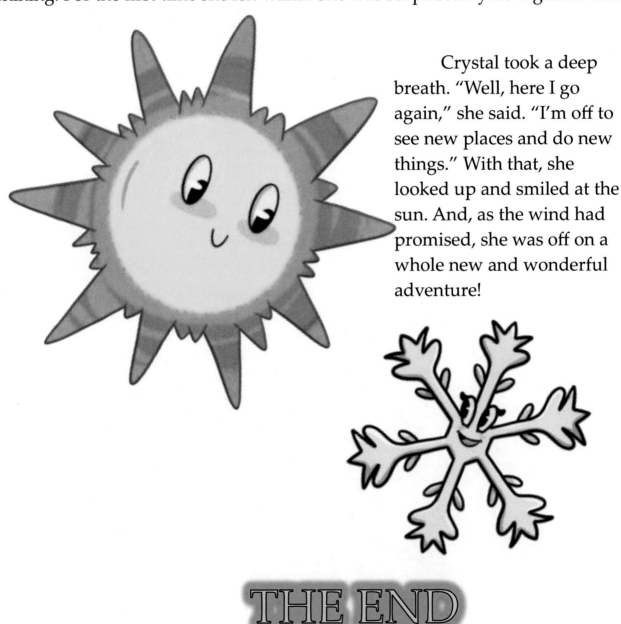

Crystal took a deep breath. "Well, here I go again," she said. "I'm off to see new places and do new things." With that, she looked up and smiled at the sun. And, as the wind had promised, she was off on a whole new and wonderful adventure!

THE END

About the Author

S. Brent Farley is a noted educator, author, and lecturer. For 40 years he taught thousands of students of all ages and chaired committees producing student and teacher manuals used in classrooms throughout the world. He delights in storytelling and hopes to have a positive influence on as many young readers as his stories can reach. He resides with his wife Janene in Gilbert, Arizona.

Other books by S. Brent Farley

Sammy the Seahorse

Fun Poems For Children

Upcoming books by S. Brent Farley

The Fiery Dragon of Thunder Mountain

The Crazy Zoo in Timbuktu

Made in the USA
Monee, IL
10 October 2020